Gridiron Grit © 2023 by North Star Editions, Mendota Heights, MN 55120. All rights reserved. No part of this book may be used or reproduced in any manner whatsoever, including internet usage, without written permission from the copyright owner, except in the case of brief quotations embodied in critical articles and reviews.

Book design by Sarah Taplin
Cover design by Sarah Taplin
Cover images by Shutterstock Images

Published in the United States by Jolly Fish Press, an imprint of North Star Editions, Inc.

This is a work of fiction. Names, characters, places, and incidents are either the product of the author's imagination or are used fictitiously, and any resemblance to actual persons living or dead, business establishments, events, or locales is entirely coincidental.

Library of Congress Cataloging-in-Publication Data (pending)
978-1-63163-666-0 (paperback)
978-1-63163-665-3 (hardcover)

Jolly Fish Press
North Star Editions, Inc.
2297 Waters Drive
Mendota Heights, MN 55120
www.jollyfishpress.com

Printed in the United States of America

GRIDIRON GRIT

Mendota Heights, Minnesota

TABLE OF CONTENTS

CHAPTER 1: OFF THE BENCH 6

CHAPTER 2: THE NEW QB 12

CHAPTER 3: MEETING TRISH 18

CHAPTER 4: THE FIRST PRACTICE 23

CHAPTER 5: BRONSON'S BETRAYAL 28

CHAPTER 6: THE SEASON SOURS 33

CHAPTER 7: THE DISCOVERY 40

CHAPTER 8: SECOND-STRING STING 47

CHAPTER 9: CAM-AIR AND MEGA-BRON 54

CHAPTER 10: THE FINAL DRIVE 58

THAT'S AMAZING! DOUG WILLIAMS 68
GLOSSARY 70
ABOUT THE AUTHOR 72

CHAPTER 1
OFF THE BENCH

"You okay, Bron?" Cameron Carter asked, knowing his former best friend wasn't.

"My shoulder," Bronson Troy said. He bit down on his mouth guard, eyes welling with tears. The Northwood Middle School Lumberjacks' top receiver had just run a perfect route. Despite being double-teamed, he'd collected 27 yards on a toe-tapping catch, before getting shoved out-of-bounds inside the South Shore Swampers' 30-yard line.

"Down here, you two," Coach Reese said. He was just up the sideline, focused on giving the next call to the team's star quarterback, his daughter, Trish.

Played at night under the lights, the forty-fifth annual rivalry game was tied 7–7. The Lumberjacks were driving with 3:06 left in the fourth quarter. The winner would display the trophy—a log etched with each year's results—at their school for the year.

The grandstands were packed. Everyone was on their feet. Cowbells and air horns put an exclamation mark on play after play.

Cameron had seen Bronson get leveled and bounce back up. But he must've landed just right—or in this case, wrong.

Bronson winced and rubbed his arm.

"Coach, I think Bron—" Cameron began.

"Same play," Bronson said. He braced his left arm close to his body, pretending to study his play wristband.

"What do you think, Carter?" Coach Reese asked. After a rough start to the season, the first-year coach relied heavily on Cameron's football knowledge.

"They're getting tired," Cameron said. "And the double-team is starting to sag."

"All right," Coach Reese said. "Tampa Bay; sprint right, sixty-three comeback."

"Flip-flop sides," Cameron said. He knew that if Bronson couldn't get both arms up, he might still be able to make a one-handed grab with his good one.

When Bronson broke from the huddle,

he was visibly favoring his right shoulder. He split out far right, on the opposite side.

"Blue Twenty-Two!" barked Trish. "Blue Twenty-Two! Hut!" She took the snap and sprinted to her right. Bronson darted upfield, then broke a few yards back toward the sideline. Trish delivered a well-placed throw on his outside shoulder.

Bronson lifted his good arm to make a one-handed grab. The ball came in hot, though. It ricocheted off his shoulder pad. Bronson lunged at the suspended ball just as the defense swarmed. It fell incomplete.

When the pile cleared, Bronson was writhing on the ground. The referee blew his whistle. Coach Reese sprinted to Bronson.

"What do you think, Cam?" Trish called.

"Empty backfield. Split Simon out," Cameron said. "Replace Bron with Landon."

Bronson got to his feet gingerly. Coach aided him, stabilizing the injured arm.

"Cameron, get in there for Bronson," Coach Reese called.

"Wait, what?" Cameron stammered.

"I'm not taking your advice on this one." Coach pointed to the huddle. "Get in at *split*."

CHAPTER 2
THE NEW QB

Months earlier...

Cameron and Bronson jumped when Mr. Carter turned on the kitchen light.

"What are you boys doing up so late?" quizzed Cameron's dad. He was just as surprised to see them at the table, huddled around a laptop.

"Trish Reese," sighed Cameron.

"Who?" his dad replied. He rummaged through the pantry for a midnight snack.

"My QB competition," Cameron said. The best friends were hours into a deep dive of her social media. They hadn't expected the summer's last sleepover to go like this.

"Pfft, what are you talking about, Cam?" said his dad. He tossed a bag of popcorn into the microwave. "Didn't your mother and I just watch you two nearly single-handedly win the seven-on-seven tournament?"

Besides being best friends, Cameron

and Bronson were a lethal quarterback and receiver combination. They'd been playing together forever, and it was a given that they'd be starting—and starring—for the Northwood Lumberjacks.

"Remember that girl from the skills competition, Mr. Carter?" Bronson asked.

Mr. Carter paused for a second, then his eyes widened. "That Trish Reese," he said.

Last fall, Cameron had made it to the finals of the Great Lakes Football Skills competition. There, he ran into the force that was Trish Reese.

"Yyyuup," Cameron said. He searched for one of her viral videos. "She even has a nickname now—Triple Threat."

On cue, thumping music began, ushering in an epic highlight reel. Trish was throwing a perfect spiral to her receiver in the corner of the end zone. Then she was slicing through a defense with ankle-breaking moves. That was followed up by trick passes through a spinning tire hanging from a tree, a flaming ring in motion, and more. Then she was kicking field goals blindfolded and punting with marksman-like accuracy. It ended with her as a representative for the skills competition at the Super Bowl.

"Do you want your mother to dig out your old hula hoop and some lighter fluid?" Mr. Carter asked, trying to lighten the mood. He offered some popcorn to the boys.

"C'mon, Dad," Cameron said, stuffing popcorn into his mouth to hide a smile.

"So, how do you know this Trish Reese is going to Northwood?" Mr. Carter asked. "Was she there yesterday?"

"No, it was just her dad," Cameron said. "He told us he was our new coach."

"Maybe someone from South Shore is trying to punk us," Bronson suggested.

"Yeah!" Cameron said. He hoped it was a prank from the rival middle school. "Maybe Coach Johnson will be there after all."

Coach Johnson, longtime gym teacher and coach of the middle school football team, had recently retired. No one had heard who his replacement would be.

"If she shows, you go out and give one hundred percent," Mr. Carter said. "If she doesn't, you go out and give one hundred percent. You play like you practice, boys."

CHAPTER 3
MEETING TRISH

Cameron, Bronson, and Simon Long, who played running back, were biking to Northwood Middle School. The first day of practice was tomorrow. From afar, they saw someone throwing tight spirals into a passing net. A few others were there. One snapped pictures. Another recorded a video.

"Trish Reese," Cameron muttered.

"Guess that *was* her dad," Bronson said.

"No more Coach Johnson," Simon added. "Looks like it's Coach Reese now."

The trio sat on their bikes, watching Trish throw ball after ball into the nets.

"No way I'm catching passes from *her*," Simon snarked.

"Dude," Cameron said in disbelief. "Are you watching this?"

"She's a machine," Bronson said.

Coach Reese saw them and came over.

"You boys are a day early," he joked. He

took off his Northwood Football visor and wiped the sweat off his forehead.

"I didn't know it was media day," Simon said sarcastically.

Coach Reese didn't pick up on his tone. "Oh, yes, the *Northwood Ledger* wanted to run a story on Trish."

"Heads up, Carter!" someone shouted.

Cameron turned to see a ball headed his way. But Bronson lunged and snatched the ball right before it hit Cameron in the face.

The source of the throw was Trish Reese, and she was jogging their way.

"How do you hold the ball, Carter?" Trish said. Cameron was surprised she knew his name.

Bronson flipped Cameron the ball.

Cameron held out his hand. Trish inspected his finger placement and nodded. "I do a little something different with my pinkie, but that's close to mine," she said.

"We could use a receiver for the photo shoot," Coach Reese said.

The three boys looked at one another.

"Bronson and Simon are two of the best around." Cameron hyped his friends.

They looked at Cameron with disbelief.

"I'm going to sit this one out," Simon said. He was sticking to his boycott of Trish.

"How about you?" the *Ledger* sportswriter said to Bronson. "You didn't have any problems catching that laser she just threw."

Bronson grinned. He didn't look back at Cameron and Simon as he jogged out to the photoshoot. Cameron couldn't shake the sting.

CHAPTER 4
THE FIRST PRACTICE

Mr. Carter was reading the *Northwood Ledger* on his tablet in the living room when Cameron was leaving for practice. He handed Cameron the device.

Cameron read the headline aloud: "Triple Threat: Northwood Middle School's New

Quarterback Is Already the Star of the Team."

"Looks like you got some work ahead of you," said his dad, looking over the top of his reading glasses.

Cameron skimmed the article. "Internet sensation," "Great Lakes champion," and "superstar" were some of the words describing Trish. And that was just in the first paragraph. His own name stood out, too:

> The team isn't a complete group of strangers. Reese said she went against Cameron Carter in last year's Great

Lakes Football Skills finals, calling him "really talented."

Cameron scrolled down to a photo gallery. There were dozens of pictures: Trish decked out in a Northwood jersey with a steely glare, Bronson looking over his right shoulder, hands ready to receive what was no doubt a perfect pass.

Cameron swallowed hard.

"Always nice to see your name in print, isn't it?" Mr. Carter said, likely trying to be comforting.

But Cameron felt only nauseous.

Thirty minutes later, an airhorn blared. Standing on the giant axe at midfield was Coach Reese, the horn raised in the air. The players hustled over and took a knee around him.

"Welcome to a new era of Lumberjacks football," Coach Reese boomed. "We have some really exciting football ahead, and I know a lot of eyeballs are going to be on us."

Two TV stations, a sportswriter from the *Metro Gazette,* and a regional sports podcaster who usually covered college football were clamoring for a glimpse of, and hopefully a chat with, Trish Reese.

"My family is new to the area, but we already know how important that game is against South Shore Middle School," Coach said of the rivalry game. "Sink the Swampers!"

The team hooted and hollered.

"Let's go!" Coach shouted, whipping the team into a frenzy.

"Guess you'll be catching passes from Trish," Cameron said to Simon, who shook his head.

CHAPTER 5
BRONSON'S BETRAYAL

"Didn't you say the bell rings at 8:30?" Mr. Carter asked the next morning, yawning.

"Yeah, but the playground game starts soon," Cameron said. He threw items into his backpack.

His dad sipped his coffee. "Never seen a kid anxious to get to school an hour early."

"It's one of the best parts of the day, Dad!" Cameron said. He lived for these morning playground games. If he and Bronson were teammates, there was no stopping them. When Cameron was captain, he always picked Bronson. And when Bronson was captain, he picked Cam. They'd never made a pact about it—it was just understood.

"If you say so," his dad said and watched him ride off on his bike.

Cameron got there just in time for the

picking of teams. He walked up to a gaggle of boys—and Trish. Bronson was about to make his first pick.

"Bronny!" Cameron shouted, letting his best friend know he had arrived.

Bronson smiled at Cam and nodded.

Cameron took a step toward him, but froze when he heard "Trish!"

"Daaaaanggg!" howled someone.

Cameron could feel himself blushing.

Trish walked to Bronson's team. The two exchanged a three-part fist bump.

"Cam!" Simon excitedly said.

Cameron pumped his fist, trotting to Simon's side. He brushed by Bronson, ignoring his high five. Cameron was furious. *First, he ends up in the paper catching Trish's passes, and now he's picking her ahead of me!*

"This should be fun," said Trish. She flipped the ball to Cameron.

"Yeah," he said. "I'm already having a ball!" He walked over and slammed the ball into Bronson's stomach.

"What are you doing, Cam?" Bronson said, doubling over to catch his breath.

"What are *you* doing, Bron?"

"C'mon, guys," Trish said, stepping between them. "Let's settle it on the field."

"Need to call in a news helicopter?" Cameron mocked. "Get those clicks up?"

"What's your problem?" Bronson snapped back. "Why you moping?"

Cameron stood silent.

"What would your dad have to say?"

"He'd call you a traitor!" Cameron yelled.

"Traitor?" Bronson was flabbergasted. "I'm just trying to get in some extra reps with the starting quarterback."

Cameron stormed off to school in a huff.

CHAPTER 6
THE SEASON SOURS

Northwood started the season red-hot, at 3–0. Much to Cameron's dismay, Trish lived up to the hype. She passed for seven touchdowns and ran for five more, kicked all the extra points, booted a 31-yard field goal, and averaged over 40 yards a punt.

Cameron had stood by Coach Reese throughout it all. His jersey was spotless. As the backup quarterback, he wore a ball cap and charted plays on a clipboard. He had played in every game, but only for a handoff to kill the clock, or to kneel to end the game.

In the first three games, the Lumberjacks had scored on the first play. All were long passes to Bronson.

"Let's see if we do it again," Coach said to Cameron as they prepared to take on the Hay River Haymakers, their first real test.

"Triple Threat! Triple Threat!" shouted

the large Northwood fan section. Fans wore homemade jerseys of Trish's No. 3, the numbers made of duct tape. Phones recorded the field as Trish ushered out the offense.

Trish broke the huddle, sauntering to the line. She wiped her right hand on the towel tucked into her waistband. Then she blew into her hand, assessing the defense.

"Diamond! Diamond!" shouted the Haymakers' brawny middle linebacker, before Trish even called the signals.

Trish took the snap, retreated seven steps, looking to hit Bronson on a flag. He ran a good route, but Hay River's defense was positioned perfectly. The pocket collapsed. Trish had nowhere to go. She threw away the ball to avoid the sack.

"Get to the line!" Trish ordered, calling for no huddle. She wiped her right hand on the towel and got under center. Then she dropped back to a pistol formation.

"Coal! Coal!" growled the linebacker.

"Blue Fourteen!" Trish yelled, directing the line to which side she was running.

Bronson tapped the outside of his helmet. This let Trish know he would try to block his defender inside. Hopefully, she could make it around the corner.

"Blue Fourteen! Hike!" She dropped back, faking the pass before looking to run. The defense didn't fall for it, filling gaps and staying home. Trish lost two yards.

Trish and Bronson ran to the sideline.

"How do they know what we're doing, Cam?" asked Bronson.

Cam ignored him, focusing on his charting. He'd barely spoken to Bronson following the playground dustup. But he hated to be on a losing team.

"What about a slant?" Cam suggested. The route was their go-to when they needed sure yardage—when Cam was still starting.

"I don't know," said a frustrated Trish. "They're clogging the middle of the field."

"Yeah, they'll jump that," Bronson said.

"How about a comeback?" Trish said.

Bronson nodded in agreement.

Cam gritted his teeth.

"Eighty-Five Comeback," Coach said, blocking his mouth with his play sheet.

Yet again, the Haymakers had the route covered and nearly intercepted the pass.

Cameron couldn't believe how dominant they were. Hay River was good, but not that good. *They know something*, he thought.

It was much of the same the rest of the game. The lone Lumberjacks touchdown was an acrobatic one-handed catch by Bronson in the back corner of the end zone. Trish missed her first extra point of the season, but she made up for it with a 33-yard field goal late in the fourth quarter. The Lumberjacks were lucky to come away with a hard-fought 9–7 victory. Cameron never even got to put his helmet on.

CHAPTER 7
THE DISCOVERY

Cameron's face was beet-red, and he was drenched in sweat. Music blared from the speaker as he jumped rope. He didn't hear his dad knock or enter the room.

"Nice footwork!" Mr. Carter shouted.

Startled, Cameron turned off the music.

"Your phone is going off," said his dad.

"I'll check it later," Cameron said. He began jumping rope again. He figured it was probably Bronson, Trish, or Simon. Most of the team was meeting to break down the game and eat pizza.

"Go watch film with the team, Cam," said his dad as he shut the door.

Cameron finished his last few reps. He grabbed his laptop and plopped down onto his beanbag chair that looked like a football.

Though he wasn't playing that much, Cameron doggedly continued to prepare as if he were. He knew the playbook inside and out. Coach recognized this, making Cameron a backup at nearly every position.

Cameron looked through the game tape for some clue as to how Hay River seemed to know what play was called. Suddenly, it leapt out at him. He quickly rewound the play and watched it again. He jumped over to the games prior. It was more of the same.

He hopped up and sprinted upstairs to his parents. They gave him a perplexed look as he came barreling into the kitchen.

"Trish is tipping plays," Cameron said, before gasping to catch his breath.

"What?" Mrs. Carter was dumbfounded.

"I just realized it," replied a winded Cameron. "I looked at the first three games—she's done it the whole season."

"Wow . . ." His dad was stunned.

"And since so many videos of our games are out there . . ."

"There is no shortage of film for teams to study," said his dad, finishing the sentence.

Cameron sat down with his laptop and pulled up the videos. It was obvious, once pointed out. When a pass was called, Trish walked to the line, wiping her hand on the towel and then blowing into her right hand. When it was a run, she only wiped her hand.

"Clear as day," exclaimed Mr. Carter.

"Every time," said Cameron.

Fast-forwarding through plays, he and his dad took turns calling "pass" or "run."

"So, when are you going to tell Coach Reese?" his dad asked.

Cameron looked away. As much as he tried to be a good teammate, he was still mad about the season. *Maybe if Trish continues to tip plays and the team loses the next game or two, Coach Reese will have to play me.*

"Cameron," his mom warned.

"I will," he said, avoiding eye contact.

"It's funny," his dad said. "I had a similar thing happen when I was in high school."

Cameron's dad had been a lineman during his playing days, and he could still fill a doorframe.

"What happened?" Cameron asked.

"Well," his dad said. "I was second-string, and the starter was tipping plays."

"How?" Cameron asked, eagerly.

"When we'd run, he'd be in his three-point stance, fingers down on the ground," his dad said, getting down and demonstrating. "On passes, his down hand was barely touching a blade of grass."

"Did you tell the coach right away?" Cameron asked.

"I didn't, and it took our quarterback nearly getting his head taken off before I did," his dad said regretfully.

"What happened when you did tell?" Cameron asked. He hoped that the intel somehow got his dad a starting spot.

"He kept his starting spot, and I kept the bench warm," his dad joked.

CHAPTER 8
SECOND-STRING STING

Trish wiped her hand on the towel and walked toward the line of scrimmage. It was the Lumberjacks' first offensive play of the game, on their own 36-yard line.

"Robbers!" bellowed the entire sideline of the opposing Great Rapids Evergreens.

Trish audibled to a pass, looking to set up Bronson on a quick slant. She wiped her hand on the towel and blew into it. The Great Rapids sideline screamed, "Cops!"

"Timeout!" shouted Trish as the opposing team adjusted its field position once more.

Coach Reese waved the Lumberjacks over to the sideline. Trish was the first to get there. She was rattled, kicking the ground in front of her. "What should I do, Dad?"

Cameron had never heard her say "Dad."

"We're gonna play our game, okay?" Coach said, trying to encourage the team.

Cameron sheepishly stood a few feet away. During the week, he'd convinced himself he didn't need to alert Coach. *Great Rapids never plays well. Trish could tell them what play was coming, and she'd still do fine.*

His parents never asked him if he had told Coach. Each time he saw or even thought about them, it gnawed at him.

"Trish is tipping plays," he blurted out.

The entire offense turned and looked at him.

"She's tipping every offensive play," he said, stepping into the middle of the huddle.

"When it's a run, she wipes her hand on her towel. When it's a pass, she wipes her hand on the towel and then blows into her hand."

"Wait, what?" Coach said.

Cameron repeated himself. The team was thunderstruck.

The referee blew the whistle, telling the Lumberjacks to return to the field.

"We need a play!" Simon urged.

"Never mind," Trish said. "I got one."

The Lumberjacks ran onto the field and huddled up. The position players then scurried into a four-wide, single-back formation.

Trish walked to the line, wiping her hands on the towel and blowing into her hand.

"Cops!" shouted Great Rapids once again.

Trish stepped back and called an audible.

"Red Thirty-Four! Red Thirty-Four!" she barked, while wiping her hand on the towel. She stepped back to the line.

"Robbers!" bellowed Great Rapids.

Trish took the snap and turned to Simon with the ball extended in her hand. At the point of exchange, Trish tucked the ball into her stomach and kept her back to the play.

Hunched over as if he had the ball, Simon

sprinted toward the guard and tackle. The defense fell for it. Linemen and linebackers swarmed on the line of scrimmage. Even the free safety went to pile on.

Bronson sprinted toward the Great Rapids defensive back who was covering him face up. Bronson raised his arm like he was about to block, before ducking toward the defensive back's inside shoulder. From there, he broke out downfield in a full sprint.

Trish turned back to see Bronson streaking downfield. The defensive back, now in pursuit, was 10 yards behind. Trish squared up her body and let go a rocket. Bronson caught the ball in stride on the Evergreens' 43-yard line and kicked it into another gear. The defender never even got close.

The Lumberjacks sideline erupted. Trish pumped her fist and pointed at Cameron, before galloping downfield to celebrate with Bronson and their teammates. Cameron caught himself smiling and running to join the team. Then he saw Trish do her now-signature fist bump with Bronson. Cameron stopped in his tracks and watched the two triumph together, without him.

CHAPTER 9
CAM-AIR AND MEGA-BRON

Pointing out Trish's tendencies completely changed the direction of the season. Trish returned to form. She passed, ran, and kicked the Lumberjacks to victory.

Bronson was gaining digital traction of his own. The one-handed touchdown catch against Hay River went viral on Trish's feed. He got a nickname of his own: "Mega-Bron." Cameron spent nights watching the videos of Bronson. He felt proud at first, but then the pride turned sour. And he couldn't bring himself to ever say "Mega-Bron."

Meanwhile, Cameron's sideline duties expanded. Coach Reese often turned to him for advice. He'd helped so much with passing, the team called his brain "Cam-Air."

After routing Great Rapids 35–7, the Lumberjacks went on to shut out Copper Ridge and Clavin by matching scores of

28–0. This set up the showdown with South Shore. Both teams were undefeated.

Neither Northwood nor South Shore could get anything going in the first half. Much of the scoreless half was played between the 40-yard lines. Trish, Bronson, and the rest of the Lumberjacks offense were stopped by the Swampers shutdown cornerback, Davis Germain, and rock-solid free safety, Kenny Dodson.

There was a quick burst of scoring to start the second half. Davis returned the opening kickoff for South Shore on a reverse, fooling

Northwood. Trish responded with a long drive that ate up much of the third quarter. She capped it off with a 3-yard quarterback draw. Her extra point flew through the uprights, tying the game at 7–7.

The battle in the trenches resumed, and the game was a back-and-forth chess match until late in the fourth quarter. Northwood took possession on a South Shore miscue. The Lumberjacks drove deeper inside Swampers territory for the first time all game on the play Bronson suffered his shoulder injury.

CHAPTER 10
THE FINAL DRIVE

"Cameron, get in there for Bronson," Coach Reese said.

"Wait, what?" Cameron stammered.

"I'm not taking your advice on this one." Coach pointed to the huddle. "Get in at *split*."

"Split?" replied a stunned Cameron.

"It was Bronson's idea," Coach said.

"You know the position just as well as me—maybe even better," Bronson said, extending a fist to Cameron.

Cameron was shocked. He'd assumed all this time that Bronson had forgotten about him. He'd assumed Bronson hadn't noticed how much he'd been picking up on the sidelines. And he'd assumed their friendship was over for good. In an instant, Cameron realized just how wrong he'd been.

Cameron looked at Bronson, then extended his own fist. "I got your back,

Mega-Bron." The two friends grinned at each other for the first time all season.

Coach let them enjoy the moment. Then he returned to the huddle. "Let's eat some clock and set up Trish for a field goal."

Cameron stretched the field, lining up several yards from the sideline. Bronson stood beside Coach Reese just feet away.

Davis grinned when he lined up across from Cameron. "You gonna get that jersey dirty?" he teased.

Kenny wasn't paying any attention to Cameron either, masking Trish instead.

Trish gained seven yards on a trap. She made something out of nothing, juking Davis, who had dismissed Cameron right away. Cameron purposefully loafed to the second line of defense to block. He never reached Kenny, who had his eyes on Trish, making a beeline for the ball.

"Huddle!" Trish clumped her hands together, gathering the team.

The seconds ticked away.

"What do you think, Cam?" Trish asked.

"Same formation," replied Cameron. "Motion Landon for a jet sweep."

"Milk the clock!" Coach Reese shouted as the time dropped below a minute.

Cameron sprinted out wide. Again, Davis barely gave him a look. The talented defensive back cheated closer to the backfield. When he saw Landon in motion, he shuffled in a few steps, exploding on the snap. Davis blew up the play at the line of scrimmage. Then Kenny breezed by Cameron on his way to the action.

It was now third down and three on the Swampers' 23-yard line.

"Time-out!" shouted Coach Reese.

The Lumberjacks gasped for air and drank from water bottles.

"Still feeling the field goal?" Coach asked.

No one responded.

"What are we seeing?" Coach probed.

Silence.

"QB trap," instructed Coach. "Trish, set yourself up in the middle of the field."

"They're ignoring Cam," Bronson said. His arm was now in a sling.

Cameron had noticed it, too. He had baited Davis and Kenny. But both had kept their eyes in the backfield.

"Anything in Cam-Air?" Coach asked.

"Lumberjack Limited," Cameron rattled off. Then the whistle sounded, and the Lumberjacks got into the pistol formation.

Trish was three yards into the backfield. Simon was lined up beside her. Cameron went unnoticed and split out to the left.

Davis was more daring than before. He inched just a few yards away from the defensive end. Kenny cheated in farther, too.

Trish walked toward the line. "Timber! Timber!" she shouted, seeming to audible. She shuffled away from the center.

The Swampers defense was totally confused by Trish's motion away from the ball.

"Wildcat!" Davis shouted. He and Kenny crowded the line even more.

"Go!" yelled Trish, who was now lined up behind the right tackle.

Simon took a direct snap. He bolted to the left, toward Cameron, who took one step off the line, then broke into the backfield. Cameron ran directly for Simon's outside shoulder. As they crossed paths, Simon flipped the ball in the air.

The misdirection wasn't enough to trip

up Davis and Kenny, who were in pursuit of the ball. But when Cameron snatched the ball without breaking stride, he passed it into Trish's waiting hands as she streaked down the sideline unguarded. No South Shore defender was within 10 yards as she sprinted across the goal line.

Cameron never saw Trish score on his one pass of the season. Instead, he ended up facedown in the turf, with the Swampers' star defenders on top of him. After escaping the pile, Cameron jumped to his feet and sprinted toward the end zone. He found

Bronson and Trish and got turned around in the raucous celebration. When Cameron gathered his bearings, he was facing the bleachers. At the very top were his parents. His mom wiped tears from her eyes. His dad raised his fist triumphantly.

Cameron had hoped his quarterback skills would be needed this season, but he'd never imagined this.

THAT'S AMAZING!
DOUG WILLIAMS

In 1978, Doug Williams became the first Black quarterback to be picked in the first round of the National Football League (NFL) draft. He played five successful seasons with the Tampa Bay Buccaneers. But his low salary led him to join another football league in 1984. After that league was disbanded, Williams returned to the NFL.

He signed with Washington in August 1986. He served as the backup quarterback to Pro Bowl quarterback Jay Schroeder.

At the end of the 1987 season, Washington made the playoffs. The head coach decided to start Williams. It paid off. Williams ushered them to victories over the Chicago Bears and then the Minnesota Vikings.

On January 31, 1988, Williams started Super Bowl XXII against the Denver Broncos. He broke several Super Bowl records in Washington's 42–10 decisive victory. He completed eighteen of twenty-nine passes for 340 yards and four touchdowns. The once-backup QB earned Super Bowl MVP honors.

GLOSSARY

audible

A new play called at the line of scrimmage.

backfield

The players who line up behind the offensive linemen.

cornerback

A defensive player who covers wide receivers near the sidelines.

defensive back

A cornerback or a safety. These defenders typically cover wide receivers.

direct snap

A snap that goes to a player other than the quarterback.

formation

How an offense or defense is lined up before the start of a play.

free safety

A defensive player who does not cover a specific receiver.

in stride

Done while moving without losing speed.

line of scrimmage

The yard line on which a football play begins.

rivalry

An ongoing competition between two players or teams.

route

The path a wide receiver runs in order to get open.

second-string

Backup.

toe-tapping catch

A catch in which the receiver keeps his toes just in bounds.

undefeated

Not having any losses.

under center

Where the quarterback takes the snap right from the center's hands.

uprights

The field goal posts.

ABOUT THE AUTHOR

(Joe Niese)

Before J. N. Kelly was an author, he was an athlete. He was a fast runner who loved baseball and football. Now he gets to write about those sports. He lives in Western Wisconsin with his wife, three children, and a toy poodle.